This book belongs to .

. . . .

First published in 2014 by Miles Kelly Publishing Ltd
Harding's Barn, Bardfield End Green, Thaxted, Essex, CM6 3PX, UK

Copyright © Miles Kelly Publishing Ltd 2014

2 4 6 8 10 9 7 5 3 1

Publishing Director Belinda Gallagher
Creative Director Jo Cowan
Editor Fran Bromage
Senior Designer Joe Jones
Production Manager Elizabeth Collins
Reprographics Stephan Davis, Jennifer Hunt, Thom Allaway

ISBN 978-1-78209-486-9

Printed in China

British Library Cataloguing-in-Publication Data
A catalogue record for this book is available from the British Library

ACKNOWLEDGEMENTS
The publishers would like to thank the following artists
who have contributed to this book:
Cover (main): Estelle Corke at Advocate Art
Insides: A Montgomery-Higham

Made with paper from a sustainable forest

www.mileskelly.net   info@mileskelly.net

The Three Billy Goats Gruff

Miles Kelly

In a mountain valley beside a rushing river, there lived three billy goats. One was very small, one was middle-sized and one was huge.

The Three Billy Goats Gruff

They were called the Three Billy Goats Gruff. Every day they would eat the lush green grass by the river, and they were very content.

One day however, the Three Billy Goats Gruff decided to cross the river and see if the grass was any greener on the other side. The grass was actually no greener, nor was it really any tastier, but they all felt they would like a change.

First they had to find a way to cross the rushing river.

So, they trotted a good way upstream before they found a little wooden bridge to take them across the river.

After a supper of lush green grass, they decided to wait until the next morning before crossing the wooden bridge. They all settled down together for the night.

The Three Billy Goats Gruff

Now, what the Three Billy Goats Gruff did not know was that under the little wooden bridge there lived a very mean and grumpy troll. He could smell the Three Billy Goats Gruff, and he thought they smelled good to eat.

The next morning when the Three Billy Goats Gruff had eaten a good breakfast of green grass, the troll was still hiding under the little wooden bridge. He was waiting for his chance to have a hearty breakfast too.

The Three Billy Goats Gruff

"That little wooden bridge doesn't look too strong," said the very small Billy Goat Gruff. "I will go across first to see if it's safe," and he trotted across the little wooden bridge.

Story time

But when he was only halfway across, the mean and grumpy troll leapt out of his hiding place with a growl.

"Who is that trit-trotting across my bridge?" he roared. "I'm going to eat you up!"

But the very small Billy

The Three Billy Goats Gruff

Goat Gruff wasn't ready to be eaten up just yet. He bravely said to the mean and grumpy troll, "You don't want to eat a skinny, bony thing like me. Just wait till my brother comes across, he's much bigger." And with a skip

Story time

and a hop, the very small
Billy Goat Gruff ran across
the bridge to the lush green
grass on the other side.

The middle-sized Billy Goat
Gruff started to cross the
little wooden bridge. But
when he was only halfway

across, the mean and grumpy troll leapt out from under the bridge and roared, "Who is that trit-trotting across my bridge? I'm going to eat you up!"

But the middle-sized Billy Goat Gruff wasn't ready to be

eaten up just yet either. He bravely said to the mean and grumpy troll, "You don't want to eat a skinny, bony thing like me. Wait till my brother comes across, he is even bigger." And with a skip and a hop, the middle-sized Billy

Goat Gruff ran across the bridge to the lush green grass on the other side.

Now, the huge Billy Goat Gruff had been watching all the time. He smiled to himself and stepped onto the little wooden bridge. By this time the troll was very hungry, and he was feeling even meaner and grumpier than usual because he was so hungry.

The troll didn't even bother to hide under the bridge. He stood right in the middle of it looking at the huge Billy Goat

Gruff, who came trotting towards him. "Who is that trit-trotting across my bridge?" roared the troll. "I'm going to eat you up!"

"Oh no, you won't!" said the huge Billy Goat Gruff, and he lowered his head. With his

huge horns he butted the
mean and grumpy troll into
the rushing river. The water

carried the troll far away, and
he was never seen again.

The Three Billy Goats Gruff
lived happily for many more

years eating the lush green grass, and they were able to cross the river to get to the other side whenever they felt like a change!

The End